BIG BEN

Published in Canada by Fitzhenry & Whiteside,
195 Allstate Parkway, Markham, Ontario L3R 4T8

Published in the United States by Fitzhenry & Whiteside,
121 Harvard Avenue, Suite 2, Allston, Massachusetts 02134

Printed in Hong Kong

10 9 8 7 6 5 4 3 2 1

National Library of Canada Cataloguing in Publication Data

Ellis, Sarah
Big Ben

ISBN 1-55041-679-0

I. LaFave, Kim   II. Title.

PS8559.L57B53 2001   jC813'.54   C2001-901084-2
PZ7.E4758Bi 2001

U.S. Cataloging-in-Publication Data
(Library of Congress Standards)

Ellis, Sarah.
Big Ben / by Sarah Ellis ; illustrated by Kim LaFave. –1st ed.
[32] p. : col. ill. ; cm.
Summary: Ben thinks he's too little to do anything until his older siblings
produce his first report card, grading him on all the things little brothers do best.
IBSN 1-55041-679-0
1. Brothers — Fiction. 2. Siblings — Fiction. I. LaFave, Kim, ill. II. Title.
[E] 21 2001 AC CIP

Fitzhenry & Whiteside acknowledges with thanks the Canada Council for the Arts,
the Government of Canada through the Book Publishing Industry Development Program (BPIDP),
and the Ontario Arts Council for their support of our publishing program.

Design by Wycliffe Smith

BIG BEN

by Sarah Ellis
Illustrated by Kim Lafave

For Libby, newest member of the family

—Sarah

For Cam

—Kim

Friday is report card day.

Robin is a big kid in grade five.
She gets marks for her subjects.

Joe is a big kid in grade three.
He gets comments for his subjects.

Ben is a little kid in preschool.

There are no subjects in preschool.

There are no report cards in preschool.
Dad and Mum are happy that Robin
and Joe have learned so many new things.
They put the report cards on the fridge.

For a Friday treat, everyone goes
to the swimming pool.

Robin does cannonballs.

Joe does the dog paddle.

Ben can't swim.

Then everyone goes out for supper.

Robin picks fat noodle soup.
Joe picks crispy shrimp.

Ben can't read the menu.
He can't use chopsticks.
His stomach hurts.

On the way home Robin sees a dump truck.

14

Joe sees a man walking four dogs.
Ben is too little to see.

At bedtime Ben doesn't want a song
or a story. He only wants Blanky.

Robin and Joe come
into Ben's room.

"Come with us,"
they say.
"Come into the office."

In the office Ben sits on the twirly chair.
Joe gets him a glass of ginger ale for his sore stomach.

Robin and Joe type on the computer.

They print on the printer.

They give Ben a piece of paper.

"What is it?" says Ben.

"It's your report card," says Joe.

"Does it have subjects?" says Ben.

"Yes," says Robin.
"Your subjects are:
Feeding the Cat,
Shoe Tying,
Tooth Brushing,
Whistling, and
Making Us Laugh."

"Does it have comments?" says Ben.

"Yes," says Robin.

"The comments are:

Very Good, Excellent, Superb, Superior…"

"And Totally Cool," says Joe.

"Does it have marks?" says Ben.

"Yes," says Robin.

"You can read them."

"A, A, A, A, A,"

reads Ben.

"That's right," says Joe,
"Straight A's."

25

"Bedtime!" says Mum.
Ben feeds the cat.

He whistles as he
goes upstairs.

He brushes his teeth.

He puts his report card
on his dresser.

Ben gets into bed.

He gets out of bed.

He ties his shoes.

Dad comes in to say goodnight.
"Why are your shoes tied?"
says Dad.

"Ready for the morning," says Ben.

Dad laughs and kisses Ben.
"You are a big goof."

Ben snuggles down.

"Big," he says to himself.
"Big, totally cool, straight A goof."